To my three tough girls, Tyler Jane, Jordan and Carlyn —LB

To mum, the first art teacher of my life —CM

Library and Archives Canada Cataloguing in Publication

Title: Tough like mom / Lana Button ; illustrated by Carmen Mok.
Names: Button, Lana, 1968- author. | Mok, Carmen, 1968- illustrator.
Identifiers: Canadiana (print) 20200216392 | Canadiana (ebook) 20200216406 | ISBN 9780735265981 (hardcover) | ISBN 9780735265998 (EPUB)
Classification: LCC PS8603.U87 T68 2021 | DDC jC813/.6—dc23

Published simultaneously in the United States of America by Tundra Books of Northern New York, an imprint of Penguin Random House Canada Young Readers, a division of Penguin Random House of Canada Limited

Library of Congress Control Number: 2020936951

Edited by Samantha Swenson and Jessica Burgess
The artwork in this book was rendered in gouache and colored pencils, and was edited digitally in Photoshop.
The text was set in Bembo Infant.

Printed and bound in China

www.penguinrandomhouse.ca

1 2 3 4 5   25 24 23 22 21

tundra | Penguin Random House
TUNDRA BOOKS

TOUGH Like MUM

Lana Button   Carmen Mok

tundra

I'm tough like Mum. Everyone in town says. So why is my thumb in my mouth? I yank it out before Mum sees.

Sometimes she's up, making breakfast, packing lunch. Today she's still in bed beside me.

So I get up. No milk means no spilling — and I don't need a spoon.

Just ends. So the last two pieces of pepperoni and a mustard smile.

And now I know what's for dinner! "Tomato, you are my favorite soup. Sit right here and wait for me."

I did my homework but Mum didn't sign *anything* — not even the field trip form! Next week we go on a bus to see a play, and my teacher keeps asking for my form. I *told* Mum it's due *today*! And I need six dollars, but that's not here either.

Still, no matter how much I shake, she won't uncurl. "Don't start on me, Kim!"

Her voice says, *I mean it!*

I dig in Mum's Red Rooster apron for
tip money. Just three quarters. I take
them anyway.

Because now I'm mad. My form will be late.
My teacher will give me that look.
What if I can't go on the trip?

Kids walking past means it's time to leave.
Clouds coming out of their mouths means it's cold.
    "I'm going!" I hurry to catch the crowd.

I jingle the frozen coins inside my mitt all the way to school.

"Where's your hat, Kim?" Denise's mother is giving me that look.

"At home," I tell her. "I don't need it."

"That's Jen's kid. Just as tough as her mum," James's dad winks and tugs my hood up, and I smile back.

As soon as I get to my classroom, my eyes go straight to the board.

I pass my form in anyway. With the quarters. Maybe Mrs. Jones won't notice.

Reading out loud is the best part of the day. Mrs. Jones tells everyone I use great *inflection* and *expression*. I make my face tough like Mum. But deep inside where no one sees, I'm a whole bunch of happy and proud.

Lunch is the worst. David's always got something to say. He yells so everyone hears, "Kim's eating a *butt* sandwich!" I make my face tough like Mum. But deep inside where no one sees, I'm a whole bunch of sad and mad.

When everyone's doing math, Mrs. Jones calls me to her desk. She's got that look. And my form.

Mum *has* to sign. "But," my teacher says, "tell her to put a check in this box right here."

That's the "I can't pay" box. That box means "I need help." Mum *never* checks that box.

I'm tough like Mum. So why do my eyes sting like I might cry right here in front of everyone? I put my head down and pretend I'm doing math. I let my thumb sneak in my mouth, just till my eyes go back to dry.

Sometimes when I get home Mum is making dinner, full of funny stories about who came into the Red Rooster. But today she's at the table wearing what she slept in last night.

Mum looks . . . like she could use some soup.

I don't need the stove to make this soup taste good. I stir out all the lumps and pour two bowls.

I slide one bowl to Mum. She slides it back.

"Eat. You'll feel better." My voice says, *I mean it.*

She looks at me surprised, but I'm looking right back at her.

We have a staring contest. For a long time.
Finally someone smiles first.
Then we're both laughing. And eating soup.

I grab my book and read out loud for as long as I can see the words. I use lots of *expression* and *inflection* while Mum listens and laughs at all the funny parts.

I go to clean up. But Mum says, "I got this," and takes our bowls.

Then she jokes, like I'm a customer at the Red Rooster, "Can I get you anything for dessert?"

When I flip open my homework book, we both see the form.

My Mum looks tough — tough as I've ever seen.
She signs. And checks the box.

We're tough. But sometimes we like to lie in bed, and
whisper silly stories, and snuggle close together.
Sometimes we fall asleep like that. Me and Mum.